IN
AUNT LUCY'S
KITCHEN

THE · COBBLE · STREET · COUSINS

IN
AUNT LUCY'S
KITCHEN

CYNTHIA RYLANT

illustrated by

WENDY ANDERSON HALPERIN

ALADDIN PAPERBACKS
New York London Toronto Sydney Singapore

First Aladdin Paperbacks edition May 2000

Text copyright © 1998 by Cynthia Rylant
Illustrations copyright © 1998 by Wendy Anderson Halperin

Aladdin Paperbacks
An imprint of Simon & Schuster
Children's Publishing Division
1230 Avenue of the Americas
New York, NY 10020

Also available in a Simon & Schuster Books
for Young Readers hardcover edition.
Designed by Heather Wood
The text for this book was set in Garth Graphic.
The illustrations were rendered in pencil and watercolor.
Manufactured in the United States of America

20 19

The Library of Congress has cataloged the hardcover edition as follows:
Rylant, Cynthia.
The Cobble Street cousins : in Aunt Lucy's kitchen / by Cynthia Rylant.
p.   cm.
Summary: While staying with their aunt for a year, three nine-year-old cousins keep busy baking and selling cookies, putting on a poetry and singing performance, and trying to encourage a romance between their aunt and one of her former customers.
ISBN-10: 0-689-81711-8 (hc.)
[1. Cousins—Fiction.] I. Title.
PZ7.R982Cj.   1998   [Fic]-dc21   97-20995   CIP AC
ISBN-13: 978-0-689-81708-3 (Aladdin pbk.)
ISBN-10: 0-689-81708-8 (Aladdin pbk.)
0909 OFF

TABLE OF
CONTENTS

For Cousin Jenn

C.R.

For Cousins Mare, Lane, and Molly

W.A.H.

IN
AUNT LUCY'S
KITCHEN

THE COOKIE COMPANY

On Cobble Street in a light blue house with pretty pink curtains and geraniums by the door, there lived three girl cousins and their aunt named Lucy.

The cousins were Lily, Rosie, and Tess, and they were all nine years old. They were living with Aunt Lucy for a year because their parents—all of whom were dancers—

were touring the world with the ballet, and the three girls knew that they did not want to go to boarding school and they did not want to live in hotels all the time. They wanted to play and to live in a house.

So they lived with Aunt Lucy.

Aunt Lucy was wonderful. She owned a flower shop on the corner and every day she went to her little shop and sold flowers to all the people in the neighborhood. Even people who did not like flowers very much bought Aunt Lucy's flowers, for she was so friendly and so pretty—with her long red hair and colorful dresses— and her shop was so inviting. She even made tea for her customers.

Lily, Rosie, and Tess shared a bedroom in the attic of Aunt Lucy's house. It was a very large attic (for the house itself was large and very old and, of course, a bit drafty in winter), and each girl had her own "room" within the attic.

Lily's room, in the middle of the attic, was surrounded by long, lacy yellow curtains. Inside her curtained room she had a small wicker bed, a trunk all painted with roses (for her rabbit collection), and a small table for writing. Lily liked to write poems.

Rosie (who was Lily's sister) made her room in the south corner of the attic, near the stained-glass window which Rosie loved so well. She loved the colors of the glass spreading all around her on sunny days. Rosie's bed was tucked behind an old patchwork quilt, and on her bed she kept her rag doll, Angel Girl, and her bear, Henry. And in a pretty blue suitcase beside the bed was Rosie's collection of paper dolls.

4

Tess's room was at the other end of the attic, behind a large screen painted with palm trees (from Aunt Lucy's trip to Hawaii). Tess loved music, and she had a small record player beside her bed which had been her father's when he was a boy. Tess kept a large stack of old records in a milk crate, and she played them all the time. She knew all the words to the old songs. When she grew up, Tess wanted to be on Broadway.

Tess also had a cat, which Aunt Lucy kindly let her keep. The cat's name was Elliott and he was black and white and slept on Tess's bed most of the day. The cousins all loved him. And Aunt Lucy brought catnip from her flower shop every afternoon.

The girls had moved into Aunt Lucy's attic in June, and now they had the whole summer ahead of them. Naturally they were considering what summer things they might do, and it was Lily who came up with the idea of a cookie company.

"A cookie company?" asked Tess, as the three sat dangling their legs on Aunt Lucy's front porch swing.

"Sure," said Lily. "Everybody loves cookies. We could take orders from the neighbors and deliver fresh-baked cookies right to their doors."

"Yum," said Rosie. She was holding her favorite paper doll, a Victorian girl dressed all in white with a dog in her arms.

"How do we advertise?" asked Tess.

"Lily could write a poem," said Rosie.

"Good idea!" said Tess.

Lily nodded her head.

"I could do that," she said.

"We could put the ad in Aunt Lucy's shop. And in French's Market," said Rosie.

"And on the library bulletin board," said Tess.

"Do you think Aunt Lucy will let us?" asked Rosie.

"For free cookies? Sure!" said Lily.

Lily was right. Aunt Lucy agreed to let the girls have a cookie company.

"Remember, clean hands—clean kitchen," said Aunt Lucy. "And aprons for everyone."

"We promise," said the cousins.

"I especially love Cinnamon Crinkles," said Aunt Lucy with a smile.

So Cinnamon Crinkles were the first cookies the girls baked. And they were delicious! Even Elliott thought so, for he ate up all the little pieces of dough left under the kitchen table.

"We're ready to advertise," said Lily.

She made up a poem and Tess and Rosie printed the posters:

The cousins were in business!

DELIVERIES

a few days later, the Cobble Street Cookie
Company received its first order.

Rosie answered the phone.

"Hello, is this the cookie
company?" asked a woman's
voice.

"Yes it is!" said Rosie
excitedly. "May we
help you?"

The woman asked Rosie to deliver one dozen fresh-baked Cinnamon Crinkles to her apartment on Friday. Her book club was having a meeting.

Rosie took the order, hung up the phone, and nearly fainted with delight!

Just then the phone rang again. Someone was having a birthday party. Could the company deliver some cookies?

Soon after that, the phone rang *again*. Someone was home from the hospital. Could the company make some cookies, please?

Rosie wrote down the orders as fast as she could. When finally the phone stopped ringing, she called to the girls.

"Lily! Tess! We have customers!"

The next day the cousins put on their aprons and baked all morning long. Lily was in charge of pouring the ingredients, Rosie was in charge of mixing, Tess rolled up the little balls of dough.

While the cookies baked, the girls dreamed of what they would do if the cookie company made them rich.

"I'm going to move to New York," said Tess. "I'll live in a penthouse and go to Broadway musicals every single day. And I'll have an Irish setter."

"I'd like a little cottage," said Rosie. "With flowers and a fish pond and lots of stained glass."

"I'm going to travel," said Lily. "To China or India or Africa. I'll wear flowing scarves and carry a canary and ride on trains."

Ding-ding.

"Cookies are ready!" everyone cried.

By afternoon, the cousins had four dozen cookies made and ready to deliver. They put on fresh dresses, tucked bows in their hair, and kissed Elliott good-bye.

Their first stop was the brick apartment building two blocks over on Vine Street. It was a wonderful old building with stone lions guarding the front and topiary trees.

"I'll bet there's some stained glass in this

building," said Rosie as the girls rang the buzzer for Apartment 5.

A woman's voice answered.

"Yes?"

"Cookie Company!" said Tess loudly. Lily giggled. Tess was so *professional*!

"Come right in," said the woman, and she buzzed the girls through the entry door.

The hallway floors were marble, and a beautiful fountain with cherubs stood just inside the door.

"Wow," said Rosie, letting the water splash on her fingers.

The girls smoothed down their hair and checked each other's bows, then knocked on the door of Apartment 5.

Presently the door opened and a very tall woman in a suit and high heels smiled at them. She had large gold earrings and very red lipstick.

"Wonderful!" she said. "Do come in."

The cousins stepped into Apartment 5. They passed through a narrow foyer, then out into the living room.

"Wow," said Rosie again.

The living room really was a *living* room, for it was filled with enormous indoor plants. Tall tropical trees raised their giant leaves to the ceiling. Vines trailed across windowsills. Cacti bloomed with scarlet flowers. There were even orchids growing on a window seat.

19

On one of the sofas sat a young man with his leg in a cast. He was thin and looked tired about the eyes, but he gave the girls a sweet smile.

"Cinnamon Crinkles," he said. "After two weeks of hospital food, they're just what I need."

The cousins smiled. None of the girls knew what to say, even Tess. They were all so impressed by everything.

"This is my brother, Michael," said the woman in the suit.

"How do you do," said Lily with a curtsy. Rosie stared at Lily. Where did Lily learn to do *that?*

Tess found her voice.

"I'm Tess, this is Rosie, and that's her sister, Lily. We're cousins and we live with our Aunt Lucy on Cobble Street."

The woman and her brother smiled at the girls.

"How nice to live with one's cousins," said the woman.

"Yes," said Rosie. "We have rooms in the attic. My room has stained glass."

"Oh, I love stained glass," said the woman. "We have a lovely stained-glass window in the kitchen."

"You do?" Rosie said excitedly.

"Yes," said the woman. "You can bring the cookies in the kitchen and while I get my purse, you can admire the glass."

"Oh, good!" said Rosie.

"By the way, my name is Mrs. Haverstock," said the woman as she and Rosie walked toward the hallway.

Lily and Tess stood shyly in the living room, their eyes following the trees to the ceiling.

"The ceilings in this building
are fifteen feet tall," said Michael.
"I'm thinking of installing a
giraffe to go with my trees."

The girls giggled.

"How did you break your
leg?" asked Tess. Lily nudged her
in the side for her bad manners. Lily had
been taught never to ask personal questions.
But Tess was so out-going, she asked
everyone everything.

"I am embarrassed to say that I fell off a ledge," said Michael.

"Really?" said Tess, who was a bit clumsy herself and glad to meet another stumbler.

"Yes, believe it or not, it was at the art museum," said Michael. "I climbed onto the ledge alongside the stairs in front of the building, to see what was in a nest, and I got so interested in what I was doing, I fell off."

"I do that all the time," said Tess.

Michael smiled.

"What was in the nest?" asked Lily.

"Baby birds," said Michael. "Swallows, I think."

Tess looked all around at the trees and plants.

"Aunt Lucy would love this place," she said.

"She enjoys plants?" asked Michael.

"*Loves* them," said Tess. "She owns Lucy's Flowers on the corner of Cobble and Plum."

"*That's* your Aunt Lucy?" asked Michael.

"Yes," Lily and Tess answered together.

"Do you know her?" asked Tess.

"Oh . . ." Michael hesitated. "Not really. No. I just . . . I was in a few times and . . . noticed her."

Lily and Tess glanced at each other. Michael was *blushing*!

"You should stop in the shop for tea sometime," said Tess. "Tell Aunt Lucy that we sent you."

Michael smiled.

"Well, as soon as I'm able to hobble about, perhaps I will."

Rosie and Mrs. Haverstock returned to the living room. Rosie was all smiles.

"You should see the stained glass," she said.

"We'd like to, but we have to go," said Lily. "We have one more delivery to make."

"Well, thank you so very much," said Mrs. Haverstock. "You girls are delightful."

The cousins grinned. What a good time they were having!

"Michael, don't forget Aunt Lucy!" said Tess. This time, *Lily* was blushing—at Tess's boldness.

Michael smiled.

"I won't," he said. "Good-bye for now."

Outside on the sidewalk the girls were all chatter.

"He likes Aunt Lucy!" said Tess.

"I know! I know!" said Lily. "He turned so pink!"

"What are you talking about?" said Rosie.

And on their way to the next delivery, Lily and Tess told Rosie all about Michael.

"He fell off a ledge?" asked Rosie, ever practical. "How could he fall off a ledge?"

"He's in love with Aunt Lucy and all you can wonder is how he fell off a ledge?" asked Tess dramatically.

"He should write a poem for Aunt Lucy," said Lily. "I could help him."

"Here's the house," said Tess, back to business. The girls checked the address. Yes, it was the house with the birthday party. But it seemed rather quiet for a birthday. There were no cars parked in front. No balloons on the door. Just a small pink house with organdy curtains and an umbrella by the front door.

The girls walked onto the porch and rang the bell.

They waited and waited and waited, and just as Tess was about to ring again, the front door slowly opened.

And there stood a very old woman. She was rather hunched and very frail, but she had beautiful white hair and sparkling blue eyes.

"Ah," she said sweetly, "birthday cookies. Please come in."

The cousins quietly and politely stepped inside the door. The house was dark and silent and smelled faintly of lavender.

"I am Mrs. White," said the elderly woman, shaking hands with each girl. "Please come in and sit down while I get your money."

While the cousins walked over to a long

velvet sofa in the living room, Tess introduced herself and Lily and Rosie. They waited as Mrs. White searched in a drawer for her coin purse.

"Whose birthday is it?" asked Tess. Lily nudged her in the side.

Mrs. White, purse in hand, turned to Tess and smiled.

"Why, it's mine, dear," she answered. "I am ninety years old today."

The cousins gasped.

"Ninety years old!" cried Lily. "Oh my goodness!"

"Yes." Mrs. White sat down in a wing chair and smiled at the girls.

"Are you having a big party?" asked Tess. Lily nudged her again.

"Oh no, dear," said Mrs. White. "Just myself. My only son passed away last year. And, well, at ninety, it's rather difficult to make new friends." She smiled. "I don't travel far these days."

Rosie, who had the most tender heart, said at once, "Then we will sing you 'Happy Birthday.' Would that be all right?"

"I'm a *very* good singer," added Tess.

Mrs. White smiled shyly.

"That would be lovely," she said softly.

The cousins stood up, smoothed their dresses, and sang.

When they were finished Mrs. White had tears in her eyes. She applauded them.

"Beautiful," she said. "And Tess, your voice *is* very good."

Tess beamed.

Mrs. White counted out three dollars in coins for the girls.

"Thank you very much for the birthday cookies," she said, handing them the money.

"They're free," blurted Rosie. Lily and Tess looked at her in surprise.

"Oh no, dear, please, I do want to pay for them," said Mrs. White.

"No, no," said Rosie sincerely, her eyes wide. "Please let us give them to you for your ninetieth birthday. We've never known anyone who was ninety. Please let us."

Mrs. White looked at Rosie's pleading face. She smiled and put the coins on the table.

"All right, my dear," she said. "But you must let me give each of you one of my little cats."

"Cats?" said Tess. "Oh, we couldn't, Aunt Lucy said only one cat at home and . . ."

"Not real cats, dear," said Mrs. White. "I'll show you."

And she opened a brown wicker sewing basket beside her chair and took out a small cotton cat. It was white with little black eyes, pink whiskers, and a glittery collar.

"I love it!" cried Lily. "I have a rabbit collection," she told Mrs. White.

Mrs. White let each cousin choose the cat she most liked, and then it was time to go.

"Happy birthday, Mrs. White," said Rosie. "We hope you like the Cinnamon Crinkles."

"Thank you so much, my dears. What a lovely day you've given me," said Mrs. White, clasping each girl's hands.

"Bye!" called the cousins as they walked down the sidewalk.

Mrs. White waved to them until they turned the corner and were out of sight.

"I can't wait to tell Aunt Lucy about this day!" cried Tess.

"Me too!" said her cousins.

And they ran all the way home to bake cookies for their Friday delivery.

THE SHOW

The Cobble Street Cookie Company lasted exactly three weeks, and then it folded. Lily, Rosie, and Tess made ten dollars apiece—enough for a new rabbit for Lily, a tea set for Rosie, and

 a record for Tess. Then they took down all of the ads, for the girls were quite tired of baking and ready for something new.

"We should go visit Michael," said Lily one afternoon.

"Oh no, Lily," said Rosie. "Mother would never want us intruding."

"But he hasn't come to the shop to see Aunt Lucy yet," said Lily. "He needs a nudge."

"If you nudge him too hard, he might break his other leg," said Tess with a giggle.

"He might fall off a porch," said Rosie.

Tess and Rosie couldn't stop giggling.

"You two are so unromantic!" complained Lily. "We should *do* something!"

The cousins thought about how they might introduce Michael to Aunt Lucy.

"Why not have a performance and invite Michael and Mrs. Haverstock?" said Tess.

"What sort of performance?" asked Lily.

"A program," said Tess. "With poetry and song. Like the artists in Paris do."

"I could write a poem to read aloud," said Lily. "Maybe a poem about young lovers finding each other."

"Or falling off a bus," giggled Rosie.

"I could sing, of course," said Tess.

"Something old and romantic, sort of bluesy."

"What shall I do?" asked Rosie.

"Give a lecture on stained glass?" said Lily.

"*No.*" Rosie grinned, giving Lily a little push.

"You could be the host," said Tess. "You can welcome everyone and introduce us, like the Oscars."

"Okay," said Rosie.

"Let's find some paper and make invitations," said Lily.

The girls printed out four decorated invitations: one for Aunt Lucy, one for Michael and Mrs. Haverstock, one for Mrs. White (to be polite, for they doubted she would come), and one for Mr. French of French's Market. He was always so kind to the cousins and had

even given them two free jars of cinnamon when they were in business.

The program was scheduled for Sunday afternoon. It was called "A Collection of Classics by Comely Cousins." (It was Lily's idea. Tess wanted to call it simply "The Show," but Rosie sided with Lily.)

Aunt Lucy was very sweet in helping the girls prepare the house for company. She put pots of daisies and daylilies all around the parlor and made fresh blueberry muffins to serve with tea. She even lit candles and lined them up on the fireplace mantel.

"So *dramatic*!" said Tess.

The cousins weren't sure if anyone would come to the Collection of Classics, but at 1:45 they saw a large green car pull up in front of Aunt Lucy's house.

"It's Mrs. Haverstock!" cried Lily. "And Michael!"

The girls ran outside to greet them. Mrs. Haverstock was all dressed up and smelled of perfume. She looked very elegant, and she smiled broadly at the cousins.

"Hello again!" she called.

Michael pulled himself out of the car and

leaned on a cane. He was dressed more simply, in jeans and a sport coat. He waved shyly at the girls.

Rosie stepped up and shook Michael's hand as the other girls led Mrs. Haverstock into the house.

"Hi, Michael," Rosie said with a big smile. "How are your trees?"

"Taller," said Michael. "Just like you, Rosie. I believe you've grown."

Rosie shook her head and lifted a foot.

"Heels," she whispered. "Tess insisted."

Michael grinned, gave Rosie his arm, and walked her to the front door.

Just inside, Aunt Lucy was helping Mrs. Haverstock with her purse and jacket. Rosie glanced at Michael.

He was blushing again!

Rosie led him proudly to Aunt Lucy.

"This is my Aunt Lucy," said Rosie.

"How are you," said Michael, extending his hand. "I'm Michael Livingston."

Even his ears were red! Rosie couldn't wait to tell Lily and Tess, who were busy preparing to perform.

"Hello, Michael," said Aunt Lucy. "The girls are so happy you've come. Would you care to sit down?"

Michael looked at Aunt Lucy's old-fashioned parlor with its wicker rocking chair, its fainting couch, its old family portraits on the wall.

"I love old houses," said Michael.

"Oh, please let me give you a tour," said Aunt Lucy. "We'll be right back, Rosie."

Rosie wanted to scream as they walked away, she was so excited!

Mrs. Haverstock was in the parlor talking with Mr. French, who had just arrived. They knew each other well, for they had gone to high school together many years before. Already they were trading stories and laughing.

Aunt Lucy returned with Michael—she looked so happy!—then just as everyone was seated and Rosie was about to begin her welcome, the doorbell rang.

On the front porch was Mrs. White, holding the arm of a taxi driver.

"Mrs. White!" the three cousins called in delight. Aunt Lucy followed them to welcome Mrs. White into the house.

"I haven't seen a good show in fifty years, my dears," said Mrs. White. "I thought I'd better not miss this one."

"We're so glad you could come, Mrs. White," said Aunt Lucy. "I'm Lucy Weatherbee and, of course, you know my girls."

"Your angels," said Mrs. White with a smile. She thanked the taxi driver and followed everyone to the parlor. Michael and Mr. French both stood up and offered Mrs. White their seats.

"Thank you, gentlemen, but this small chair will do just fine," she said.

Eventually all were introduced and settled and the program began.

Rosie welcomed everyone and wished them

all a happy afternoon. Then she introduced
Lily and added, "She will one day be a famous
writer and you will be glad you saw her here."

Lily stepped forward and read a long poem
about a young woman who was lost at sea.

The poem was at first very sad, and Rosie—always the tender heart—got worried and thought she might cry. But then the young woman was found by her true love and all turned out happily. When it was time for applause, Rosie clapped hardest.

Then she introduced Tess, "one of the finest young singers this side of Broadway," said Rosie. "She will perform, especially for Aunt Lucy, a love song called 'That Sweet New Face.'"

All three girls looked at Michael: red as a strawberry!

Tess, wearing a large purple hat with feathers, stepped into the middle of the room. She took a small harmonica from her pocket, blew a few chords, then began singing. It was such a catchy tune that soon everyone in the room was tapping his feet. Mr. French had a wide

grin on his face and Mrs. Haverstock swayed
back and forth to the rhythm.

At the end of the song, Tess gave a deep
bow to the applause.

Rosie concluded the program by reminding everyone that tea and blueberry muffins would be served. Then all three cousins lined up and said "thank you and good night" in unison. Everyone applauded again.

It was a lovely afternoon. Mrs. White stayed long enough for tea but left before the others did (the same taxi driver came to pick her up). She gave each girl another little cat before she left.

Michael and Mrs. Haverstock and Mr. French and Aunt Lucy all moved into Aunt Lucy's kitchen, where they gathered around the big table and talked and talked. Lily, Rosie, and Tess—who were all ready to get out of the house and play—peeked in at them one last time.

"Aunt Lucy likes Michael, I can tell," said Lily.

"Just think, it all started in Aunt Lucy's kitchen," said Tess.

"If they get married, will he be our uncle?" asked Rosie.

The three thought a moment.

"*Yes!*" squealed Tess.

"Oh my goodness!" cried Rosie.

"*Uncle Michael!*" cried Lily.

"Isn't life with Aunt Lucy just wonderful?" said Rosie.

Then the cousins filled a plate with muffins and went out under the shady maple to make plans ... for Aunt Lucy's wedding!